Celeste Sails to Spain

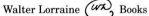

1999
Houghton Mifflin Company

Walter Lorraine WL Books

On Saturday

Clive plays football.

Nicky trains at the surf club.

Tessa has tennis practice.

Celeste goes ice-skating.   Ernie shoots baskets.   And Rosie bounces on her pogo stick.

But Frank skateboards with Roger.

At the Museum

Frank looks at the
moon rocks.

Rosie talks to Phar Lap.

Celeste makes
a rainbow.

Tessa learns how butter
is made.

Clive meets
Tyrannosaurus Rex.

And Nicky sees inside
a volcano.

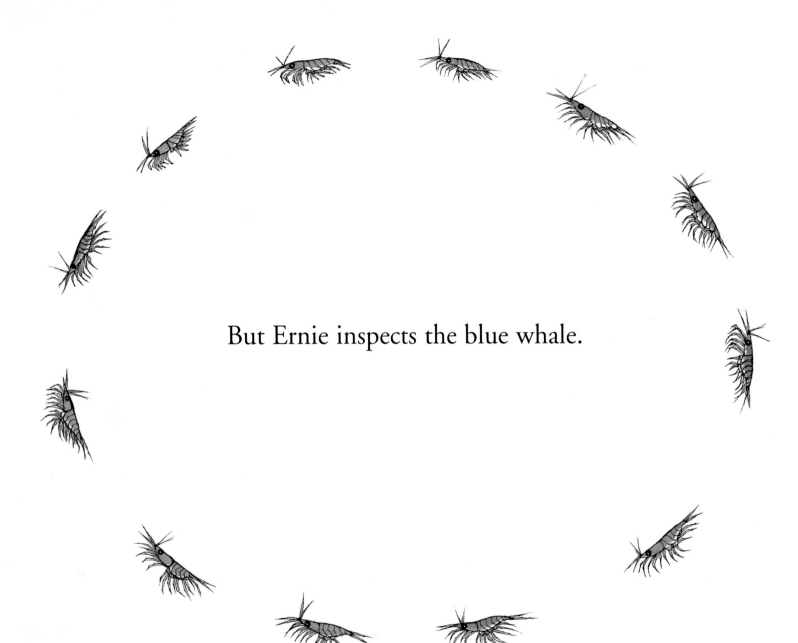

But Ernie inspects the blue whale.

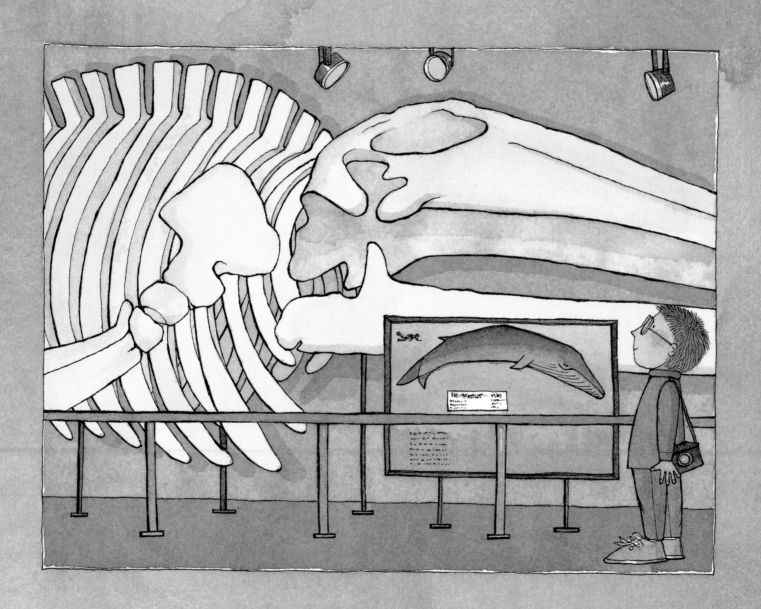

Adventures

Ernie explores a cave.   Celeste goes water-skiing.   Nicky climbs a mountain.

Rosie shoots the rapids.

Frank flies over
the lighthouse.

And Tessa dives
for treasure.

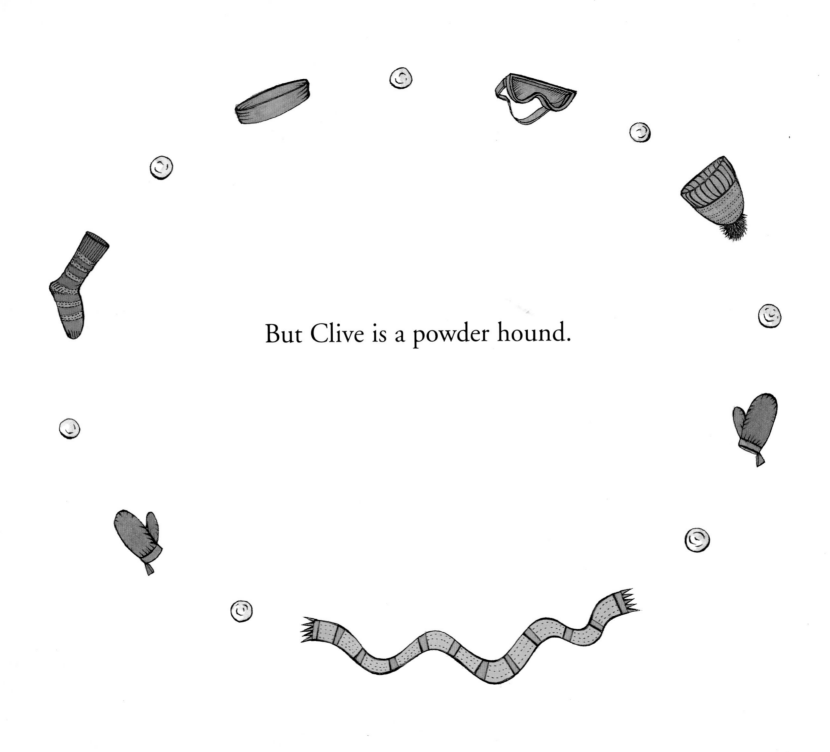

But Clive is a powder hound.

In the Park

Celeste dances with
the ducks.

Ernie has a snail race.

Tessa makes a house
of leaves.

Clive investigates
the pond.

Nicky speeds along
the path.

And Frank hides
from Roger.

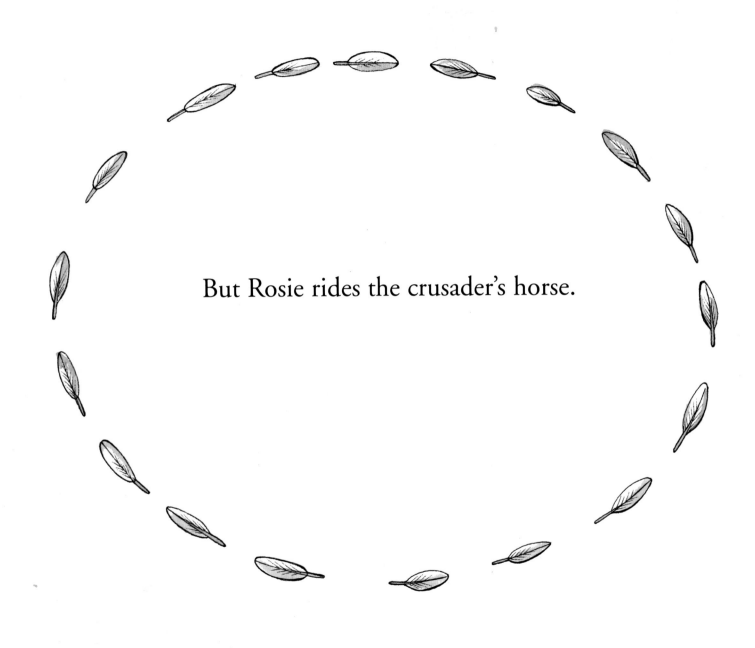

But Rosie rides the crusader's horse.

On Sports Day

Frank hurls the discus.

Nicky and Tessa run in
the three-legged race.

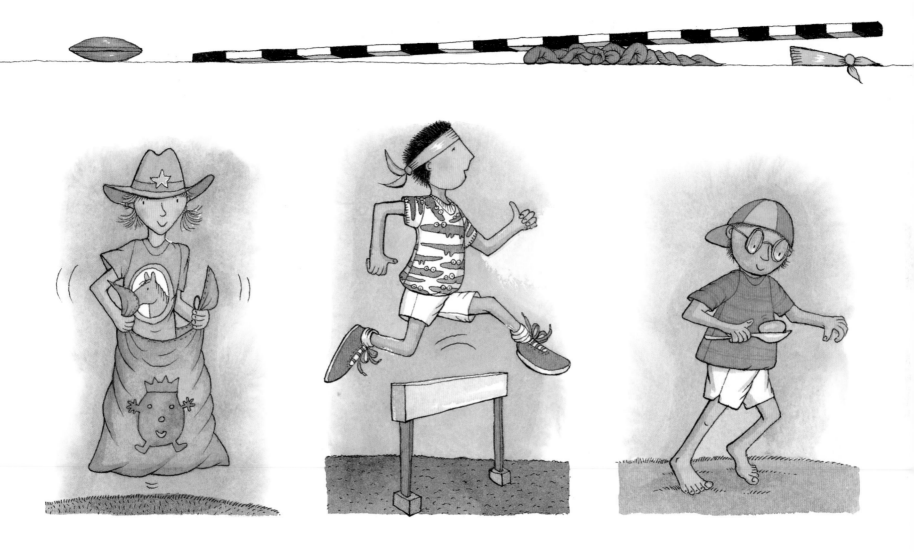

Rosie bounces in
the sack race.

Clive clears the hurdles.

And Ernie wins the
egg-and-spoon.

But Celeste flies over the high jump.

Celebrations

Celeste has a 'P' party.

Nicky trick or treats
on Halloween.

Rosie goes to a
christening.

Frank welcomes the
full moon.

Clive celebrates
Chinese New Year.

And Ernie has his
birthday at the zoo.

But Tessa runs a disco for her friends.

At the Show

Rosie rides in the
barrel race

Frank eats cotton candy.

Clive goes on the
bumper cars.

Celeste swings out on
the flying horses.

Tessa is Miss Junior
Show Girl.

And Ernie pats a pig.

But Nicky rides on the ghost train.

In Dreams

Clive goes to Kakadu.

Nicky visits the
Leaning Tower of Pisa.

Rosie rides down the
Grand Canyon.

Ernie goes to the
Galapagos Islands.

Frank views
the Pyramids.

And Tessa meets
the Queen.

But Celeste sails to Spain.

For Kate and Don

Walter Lorraine (wл) Books

Copyright © 1997 by Alison Lester
First American edition 1999
Originally published in Australia by Hodder
Headline Australia Pty Limited.

Library of Congress Cataloging-in-Publication Data

Lester, Alison.
    Celeste sails to Spain / by Alison Lester.
        p.   cm.
    Summary: Seven children enjoy a variety of activities, such as
going to the museum and having celebrations, each in his or her own
way.
    ISBN 0-395-97395-3
    [1. Individuality—Fiction.]   I. Title.
PZ7.L56284Ce   1999
[E]—dc21   98-42747
                                                              CIP
                                                               AC

Printed in Hong Kong
10 9 8 7 6 5 4 3 2 1